Welcome to the Pit!

The underground headquarters of the G.I. Joe Team is your new home. That's because you are about to become their newest member.

Your Code Name: Hotshot.

Your major talent: You work well under pressure—extreme pressure—making sure things don't explode.

Your assignment: Bomb Specialist.

A special G.I. Joe squad is about to go into action. The mission will not be an easy one. As Bomb Specialist, it will be up to you to make sure it is a *successful* one!

You will be asked to make many crucial decisions. After you do, follow the directions at the bottom of each page.

If you make the right decisions, the team will score a triumph over the evil forces of COBRA, and you will be recognized as a hero. If you make the wrong choices, you'll wish you never joined the team!

Good luck, soldier. Begin your mission on page 1.

Other G.I. JOE™ books in
the FIND YOUR FATE™ series
Published by Ballantine Books:

OPERATION: STAR RAIDER
OPERATION: DRAGON FIRE
OPERATION: TERROR TRAP

G.I. JOE

OPERATION: ROBOT ASSASSIN

BY G.V. MACRAE

BALLANTINE BOOKS • NEW YORK

RLI: $\dfrac{\text{VL Grades 5 + up}}{\text{IL Grades 6 + up}}$

Copyright © 1985 by Hasbro, Inc.
G.I. JOE$_{TM}$: A trademark of Hasbro Inc.
FIND YOUR FATE$_{TM}$: A trademark of Random House, Inc.

Library of Congress Catalog Card Number: 85-90758

ISBN 0-345-32668-7

Interior design by Gene Siegel
Editorial Services by Parachute Press, Inc.

Manufactured in the United States of America

First Edition: November 1985

Cover Illustration by Carl Cassler
Illustrated by David Henderson

FIND YOUR FATE™®

#3

G.I. JOE

OPERATION: ROBOT ASSASSIN

The door to the briefing room in the Pit closes with a "let's get down to business" slam. You're sitting by yourself, off to the side, trying to blend in. It's your first time in the G.I. Joe Command Center. The G.I. Joe Team files in and takes their seats, looking you over as if you had three arms.

"Settle down and listen up!" barks the officer at the front of the room. He's Colonel Clayton Abernathy—better known as Hawk—better known as the Joe team's head honcho.

"Within an hour, ten or twelve of you guys will be on a plane headed for Switzerland," Hawk begins. "Another round of peace talks is scheduled to begin there tomorrow. The President will be there, and so will every world leader you can name. The trouble is, COBRA, the international terrorist organization, plans to crash the party—by blowing it to smithereens."

"Colonel, should we be talking in front of the stranger?" someone asks, pointing at you.

Suddenly all eyes are on you. So much for blending in. When Hawk notices you, he calmly takes out a hand grenade, pulls the pin, and tosses it right into your lap!

Turn to page 2.

You've got to give the guys credit. When they see the grenade, they hit the floor and take cover just the way they're supposed to. But a few of them watch carefully enough to see your magic act.

You make a few quick movements with a special tool you designed yourself. Routine stuff for you—nothing to raise a sweat about. In an instant, you defuse the grenade before it blasts you into dust as fine as baby powder.

"Save your applause for the end," Hawk says, taking command of the buzzing room again. "Team, this is Hotshot. Hotshot's specialty is making sure things *don't* explode. In a minute, you'll see why Hotshot is going to be so important on this mission."

Then Hawk starts flashing slides on the screen. Aerial and land views of Geneva, Switzerland, with snow and mountains everywhere. Next come pictures of all the world leaders who are expected to attend the peace talks there.

"COBRA's gotten into the robot business," Hawk says. "We have an early report that COBRA has developed a completely lifelike and undetectable robot—programmed to kill. It's a walking time bomb with one thing on its electronic mind: Sometime during the Geneva peace talks, it's going to blow the world leaders away.

Go on to page 3.

"And there's one other small detail," Hawk continues. "We have no idea what the robot looks like. It may even be an exact duplicate of one of the world leaders. All we know for sure is that it'll look, talk, and act like a real person. We've got to find it and pull its wires before it blows."

Next Hawk starts putting together two G.I. Joe teams. "Duke, you'll lead the first team with Lady Jaye, Gung-Ho, Snake-Eyes, and Bazooka," Hawk says. "Your target is a small factory in Germany. We know the factory makes artificial legs, arms...stuff like that. But we also suspect it's a COBRA front—and the place where the robot assassin was built. Infiltrate the plant and destroy the robot—if it's still there.

"Flint, you'll take Snow Job, Airtight, Rip Cord, Mutt, and Blowtorch to Geneva. You've got to find out the robot's identity—even if it means searching every closet of every villa of every world leader staying there. And then you've got to neutralize it."

Turn to page 4.

"Hotshot," Hawk says, turning to you. "Wherever the robot turns up—you should be there. But we know you can't be in two places at once. So you get to choose. Which team do you want to join—the one that's going to Germany or the team that's covering the diplomats in Switzerland?"

It's up to you to decide!

. . . .

If you want to go to the factory in Germany, turn to page 24.

If you want to go to the peace talks in Switzerland, turn to page 80.

4

Before you can begin your ruse, COBRA begins the Crimson carpet treatment. Which means: As their special guests, you and Lady Jaye are led through a long, dusty courtyard at gunpoint. Then you're separated and hurried through an endless series of searches and metal detectors. Next, you're prodded from one dark room in the fortress to another.

Finally you and Lady Jaye meet again in a clean, well-lit room filled with telephones, radio communication equipment, computer terminals, and video monitors. But there's no time to call home.

A door opens and the Baroness and Destro enter. You take a deep breath. Fooling these two won't be easy. The Baroness is one of COBRA's top intelligence officers, and Destro is COBRA's major weapons supplier—a man so ruthless even COBRA doesn't trust him.

"You are in a secret COBRA headquarters," the Baroness says. "It's a lovely part of Spain, miles from civilization."

"Present company included," Lady Jaye says.

"Hey, I don't want to die," you say. "In fact, I'm willing to do *anything* to stay alive. How would COBRA like to have a hotshot explosives expert on their side?"

"Hotshot, you traitor!" Lady Jaye screams.

"Talk is cheap," Destro says to you.

"Quite right," the Baroness says. "Let's give him a test."

Turn to page 52.

Airtight lobs a few smoking cans in the direction of the guards at a side door. One second they're on their feet, the next second they're out cold on their backs.

Blowtorch leads the way into the building, pushing back the last group of too-eager guards with a blast from his flamethrower.

"The building's secure," Airtight says as you approach the conference room. From a glassed-in visitor's gallery, you watch the assembly below you. "The meeting has already started. Now what, Flint?"

"The way I figure, the robot must not be disguised as one of the world leaders," Flint says, squinting.

"How do you figure that, Flint?" Blowtorch asks.

"If the robot were already in there, COBRA would have blown him by now. Especially since we've arrived," Flint answers.

"You could be right," you say. "But on the other hand, the Chinese minister hasn't shown up yet. Maybe COBRA is waiting for him—so they'll get all the biggies in one boom."

"Or maybe the Chinese minister *is* the robot! Try that one on for size, guys," Snow Job says.

You must decide.

....

If you think the robot assassin is already in the conference room, turn to page 78.

If you think it hasn't arrived yet, turn to page 68.

6

"Robot? I'm no robot, you ninny," the man says.

"Lord Reg?" you ask.

"That's what my friends call me," Lord Reg says. "And who are you? You're dressed like a German peasant, but you've got a Yank's voice."

"G.I. Joe, sir," you say. "Code name, Hotshot."

"I knew everyone would be looking for me. I'm a distant relative to the Queen, you know," Lord Reg says.

"The truth is, I'm looking for a robot," you explain.

"It's all one and the same," Lord Reg says. "Those bloody COBRA chaps kidnapped me to make a robot that looks just like me. They actually plan to send this windup toy to the peace talks in my place and then blow it up right under everyone's noses."

"I know, sir. I'm here to stop it," you say.

"Well, of course it will never work," Lord Reg puffs. "Everyone there will know it's not me. It might have my face, but there's no substitute for breeding."

If you decide to go find the robot and let Lord Reg take care of himself, turn to page 23.

If you decide that first you'd better help Lord Reg get out alive, turn to page 74.

7

The President keeps saying, "I like your style, boys," over and over as you race through the halls of the embassy.

"COBRA!" Snow Job suddenly shouts.

The one word sends you flat against the nearest wall as a shower of automatic rifle fire flies past you.

"Out of our way, pests!" Blowtorch yells, returning their fire with an inferno from his flamethrower.

"That's what I like about you, Blowtorch," Rip Cord shouts as you run again. "You do everything in a big way."

"I like your style, boys," the President says.

Outside the villa, Mutt is revving the engine of a truck he's stolen. But he's not alone. COBRA agents are everywhere. You and your teammates surround the President as you climb into the truck. Mutt floors the gas, then barrels down the road, swerving to avoid crazed COBRA agents who are leaping in front of the truck wearing live mines.

Mutt doesn't let up on the gas pedal for miles.

"I like your style, boys. That was some escape maneuver. Too bad it was all for nothing," the President says with a chuckle. Then he reaches up, unscrews his head, and puts it in his lap. "You've got three seconds to live, boys," the robot's head announces.

....

Turn to page 90.

The reprogramming is a simple matter of switching a few circuit boards in the computer brain. Now the robot will awake at midnight, attach its own leg, and follow a homing signal out to destroy its *new* target—COBRA's headquarters! There's just one small problem: Where *are* COBRA's headquarters?

Lunchtime. You're sitting by yourself under a tree on the factory grounds. An old woman with a pushcart filled with scrap pots and pans comes rattling past you.

"Spare a bite of that meal?" she asks in raspy German.

You toss your sandwich over to her because you don't want her to come too close. But she doesn't go away.

"How can you eat this junk? It's all sugar and fats," the old woman suddenly says in Lady Jaye's voice.

You try not to look surprised, but it's hard.

"Don't sit there with your mouth open. What's up?" she asks.

"I've trained a homing pigeon to fly home and kill snakes. But I don't know how to find its home," you say softly.

"Leave that to us, toots," she says with a wink.

· ·

Turn to page 41.

9

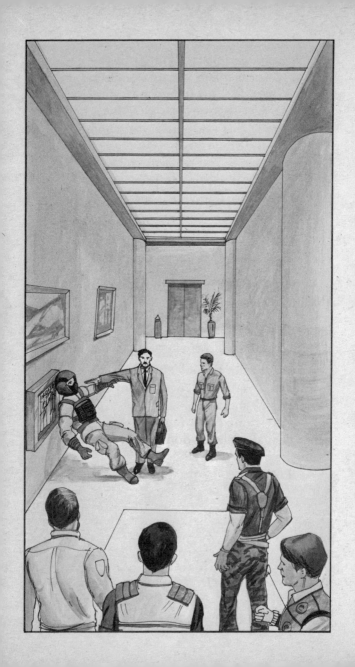

"Sorry, Doctor, no one's allowed in. We'll handle the Ambassador our way," you say.

"Maybe this will convince you differently," the doctor says. He reaches into his bag and tosses a canister at your feet. It immediately begins to smoke red.

You and the others pull back from the gas—except for one. Airtight zips up his suit and pushes his way past you. In one smooth, swift motion, he scoops up the gas canister and seals it in a lead pouch. Then, without stopping, he tries tackling the doctor. But the doctor is the robot, and he's incredibly strong! He throws Airtight against a wall.

Airtight breaks the glass to the emergency fire hose and opens the valve full blast. The force of the water jet knocks the robot off his feet. Airtight sprays him again and sends him flying around a corner.

When the deadly gas clears, you rush up to Airtight. You find him standing over a robot that now looks like a kit, batteries not included and lots of assembly required.

"Stand back, guys," you say. "This thing still might blow at any second."

Turn to page 65.

The Joe Team backs away from the door, and COBRA Commander and Destro escape with their hostage, locking you in. Snake-Eyes shatters the door with one well-focused kick, and you all pour out at a run. You come to a dead stop, however, when you find Lord Reg standing in his underwear in the middle of the factory.

"Where did they go?" Bazooka asks.

"I didn't get the chance to ask for their itinerary," Lord Reg says. "I was too busy handing over my clothes—at gunpoint."

"What did they want your clothes for?" Gung-Ho asks.

"Good heavens, that's obvious," Lord Reg replies. "English tailoring is the finest in the world."

"No offense, Lord Reg, but my guess is that COBRA Commander will use your suit as a disguise to slip out of Germany as fast as possible," says Duke. "He left you here because dragging along a hostage would slow him down."

"How am I ever going to explain this to the Queen?" Lord Reg sighs, shivering in the cold. "Oh, by the way, Hotshot. COBRA Commander asked me to relay a message to you. He said that he'll get you if it's the last thing he does. Not the most subtle chap, is he?"

"Congratulations, Hotshot," Gung-Ho says, slapping you on the back. "With a recommendation like that, it means you're really a G.I. Joe now."

THE END

In another ninety seconds, the Joe Team will assume you're in trouble and will begin a rescue mission. So you and Blowtorch scramble out of the palace as quickly and quietly as you can.

When you get back to the truck, someone new has been added to the group. Mutt is playing with a large black and white mongrel dog.

"Animals are always finding Mutt," Rip Cord tells you. "The day he was born, I'll bet his mother said, 'Look what the cat dragged in.'"

"Give it a rest, Rip Cord," Flint says. "I want to hear Hotshot's report."

"Negative on the robot," you say. "The palace is empty tonight except for El Presidente."

Turn to page 85.

You watch the action with horror.

"Is that just a dumb jerk who can't ski?" you ask Snow Job. "Or is he really zeroing in on the President of the United States?"

"He can ski, all right," Snow Job says. "I've been watching and he's in complete control. It's got to be the robot!"

When the skier is just a few feet away from the President, he suddenly falls off his skis and lies motionless on the ground. And then the worst thing happens: The President rushes over to the skier and bends down to help him. Any second now, you're going to see the robot explode—right in the President's face!

Turn to page 76.

"We'll check them all out," Flint says.

"Easier said than done," Ellie says. "The Argentine diplomats are staying in the Beuler Palace. Count Beuler built the monstrosity two centuries ago and promptly disappeared in it. The Argentines are the first people to set foot in the place in more than a hundred years. Meanwhile, the Russians are staying in the Rooster Mansion."

"I know that place," Flint says. "It's got a wall ten feet thick made of stone mixed with broken glass. You can't climb it, and you couldn't bust it with the Pittsburgh Steelers' front four."

"Behind that wall are guards and dogs," Ellie says. "And the house is full of booby traps. Maybe you'll want to try the French instead. They're staying at the Chateau Noire. It's supposed to be a ski resort, but that place is rigged with every high-tech security device known to man, and a few no one's heard about yet."

"Are you trying to scare us or make this sound like fun?" Airtight asks, picking up his gear.

Flint looks at you carefully. "You're part of the team now," he says. "What do you think, Hotshot?"

....

If you want to look for the robot in the Beuler Palace, turn to page 18.

If you want to search the Rooster Mansion, turn to page 30.

If you want to try the Chateau Noire, turn to page 36.

Using the dumbwaiter system in the kitchen, you ride up to the second floor unnoticed. The hall is a row of heavy carved doors, each with a gold skeleton key.

You unlock the first door and step into a large bedroom. The fireplace burns brightly, but the room is still cold.

You watch the fireplace for a moment and then slide your hand into the fire just the way you've seen fakirs in Delhi do. It's just as you suspected. The fire isn't burning you, and you're no fakir. It's a hologram!

Okay, there's got to be something behind the fireplace, you think to yourself. What opens this phony fireplace? A switch on the mantel? A loose brick? A swift kick?

A loose brick does it. The fireplace begins to slide forward. Then the bricks, the mantel, the whole thing falls over on top of you with a crash.

For a few minutes you're pinned by the weight of the bricks. When the world stops spinning, you stand up. What's behind the phony fireplace? A brick wall! The whole thing was just a booby-trap trick.

Wait a minute! What time is it? You check your watch. Your ten minutes in the house are up. You were supposed to meet the rest of the team outside five seconds ago!

....

Turn to page 61.

17

The Beuler Palace looks like something out of an old Dracula movie. It's surrounded by a spiked wrought-iron fence, which Blowtorch says will snap like a wishbone. But you've decided to take the place at night. The palace is a long way from the fence. In daylight, you'd be spotted running from the fence to the palace.

After dark, you and Blowtorch trade your clothes for black sweaters and pants and smear your faces and hands with black grease. The two of you are going in to search the palace for the robot assassin. The rest of the team will sit this one out—unless you're not back in fifteen minutes.

Using his low-flame laser torch, Blowtorch cuts through the bars of the iron fence in no time. The two of you slip through, and then it's a foot-race for the palace.

No guards, no searchlights, no sweat. You've reached the palace in fifty-three seconds. The servants' side door is locked, but you've brought a passkey—a small blob of plastic explosive. A little smoke, a little *pop*, and the door swings open.

"That was easy," you say.

"Too easy," Blowtorch says.

Turn to page 42.

18

Much to your surprise, it's Destro who pulls COBRA Commander off you.

"This is futile. We must save the robot!" Destro says. "It's our only chance."

But before he can make a run for it, the door blasts open. Bazooka fills the room, assuming combat position with his weapon poised on his shoulder.

"Blazing vipers!" Bazooka shouts when he sees COBRA Commander and Destro standing there. "Team, get in here on the double!"

Turn to page 81.

There may not be time to open the whole robot up and reprogram it. You could be discovered at any time. So you stuff your hand into the leg hole and begin to feel around for the explosive material. After groping around for a while, you find it. So far, so good, but you know that removing the stuff is going to be a delicate operation. Slowly and *very* carefully, you begin to ease the explosives out.

Suddenly the wall panel behind you slides open. You freeze, up to your elbow in electronics. The lights flash on, and you see Lady Jaye in the doorway. She's smiling, but pale.

"Sorry, Hotshot," she says as she's pushed toward you.

The men behind her are wearing the unmistakable red uniforms of the COBRA Crimson Guard.

"I came in as a health inspector the way we planned," Lady Jaye says. "I snooped around for a while. And then I asked a drunk, drooling man about the robot. He turned me directly over to the boys in red."

"Now what?" you ask.

"Now you go to sleep for a while," the leader of the Guards says. Three of the Guards hold you down as a fourth one gives you and Lady Jaye a very powerful anesthetic.

Turn to page 26.

You grab the COBRA agent's arms in mid-air. Falling straight backward, you flip him into a wall. That's enough to send a couple of elk heads crashing to the floor. But it isn't enough to stop *him*. When you stand up, Blowtorch is aiming his flamethrower at the COBRA agent.

"Blowtorch! No!" you shout. "Fires bring a crowd." So Blowtorch shoulders his flame-thrower like a baseball bat, swings, and hits a home run.

"I was always pretty good at hitting a screw-ball," Blowtorch says with a smile.

Too bad there's no time to reminisce about sandlot ballgames gone by. There's an old man sleeping upstairs who may be a major-league ro-bot, and you've got to snare him. The COBRA agent you just knocked out is proof enough that something's going on here in the Beuler Palace.

But when you get the old man back to the truck outside the palace, the plot sickens a little.

"He looks like El Presidente of Argentina!" Flint says.

"Whoever or whatever he is—he's fading on us," Airtight says, taking the old man's pulse. "He needs help—PDQ."

"Yeah, but a doctor or a mechanic?" Snow Job asks.

Turn to page 38.

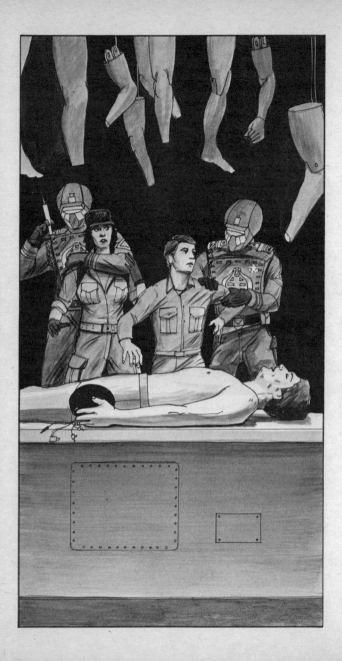

Lord Reg is safe where he is for the time being. And you've got to find the robot assassin quickly, because the peace talks begin in Geneva in thirty-six hours.

"Stay here. I'll be back for you," you say to Lord Reg on your way out. "And lock the door behind me."

You wander through the factory looking for a secret assembly shop. As you search through a storage room of artificial kneecaps, a hand grabs your shoulder.

"Hey, I've been looking for you," Lady Jaye says. "I got in disguised as a health inspector. And I've already found the robot!"

She leads you into a dark room behind a wall with no doors. You can't see very well in the dark, so you bump your head a couple of times on robotic arms and legs that hang from the ceiling on hooks.

The robot is in the middle of the room, lying lifeless on a long wooden table. Its face is an exact match of Lord Reg's. But the robot isn't finished yet. Its leg isn't connected. So you try to reach through the leg hole to feel where the explosives have been hidden.

Suddenly the lights flash on and the room fills with a red blur. You're surrounded in seconds by a squad of COBRA's Crimson Guard. Some of the Guards hold you while another gives you and Lady Jaye a very potent anesthetic.

Turn to page 26.

"Team, in five minutes we're arriving in what the tour books call a typical little German town," Duke says. "Let's get our assignments straight before we separate."

"I infiltrate the Reinhardt Robotics Factory and find out if there's a workshop where COBRA builds its robots," you say.

"I'm going to play doctor," says Lady Jaye, smiling.

"I'm going to sit in a hotel room and lose at cards to Snake-Eyes," Gung-Ho says. "I swear he learned how to see through cards on that mountaintop of his. But don't worry, we'll be there when you need us."

"Bazooka goes with me," Duke says. "We'll stay close and monitor you on radio, Hotshot. Okay, let's do it!"

First stop for you is the local inn. You've disguised yourself as a poor laborer, with dusty overalls and a beat-up hat. To hide the fact that your German is a little rusty, you play the shy, quiet type.

"I need work. Can you help me?" you say to a group of men who are sitting at a long table in the center of the room.

A burly man named Werner, who seems never to have stopped drooling since he was a baby, buys you coffee and a hard roll.

"There is work at the factory," Werner says. "No one goes hungry in this town. Drink up and I will take you there."

Turn to page 79.

"Afraid of dogs? No problem, Hotshot," Mutt says, climbing down the rope to the ground.

"Why not?" you ask.

"Because these babies aren't dogs. They're wolves!" he says with a laugh.

"Now I feel a whole lot better," you say.

Mutt doesn't wait for you. He drops to the ground, howls, and takes off on all fours.

"Will you look at that? The whole pack is following him," Flint says.

"You think we'll ever see Mutt again?" Blowtorch asks.

"Maybe next full moon," Airtight says.

The five of you slide down the rope, and Blowtorch goes right to work cutting the barbed wire on the electrified fence. "And I'd better reroute the electricity so the Russians won't know the power is down," Blowtorch says.

Before Blowtorch is through the fence, Mutt returns.

"Make any new friends?" you ask.

"I think I got proposed to," Mutt says with a laugh.

"Take her address and tell her you'll write. Get through the fence, you guys, before someone sees us," Flint says.

Turn to page 56.

There's no way of knowing how long COBRA kept you out—hours, days, weeks. When you wake up, you're blindfolded and riding in a truck down a bumpy, dusty, rut-filled road.

"Lady Jaye, are you here?" you ask.

"That's my ankle that's tied to your leg," she replies.

"We've been tied up so long I can't even *feel* my ankle," you say.

The truck suddenly stops. The blindfolds are pulled off, and you are rudely jerked out of the truck. There, in the middle of a desert, is an orange-colored clay wall. Beyond the wall is an enormous fortress. Its roof, turrets, and windows definitely look Spanish. A deserted fortress built hundreds of years ago, it has outlasted its usefulness to Spain's faded power—only to become useful again to COBRA.

"We wanted you to see the beautiful isolation of the place where you're going to die," a Crimson Guard says. You can smell "torture chambers" all over this place, so you'd better come up with a plan *fast*.

If you decide to pretend to join COBRA Forces, turn to page 5.

If you'd rather play it cool and see what COBRA has in store for you, turn to page 34.

The site of the peace talks is surrounded by soldiers in the uniforms of all nations, a colorful reminder of what world peace could mean.

But in an instant that proud image is ruined. One face stands out, hideously out of place. Major Bludd, COBRA Commander's right-hand man, is pointing at your truck and giving orders to the captain of the guard.

"COBRA has infiltrated the guards!" Flint shouts just as the guards open fire on you.

"Looks like we're not getting in this place on our good looks alone," Snow Job says.

"That was always out of the question in your case," Airtight replies, squeezing off a few rounds.

"Keep them busy, but lay off the heavy artillery," Flint says. "Remember, the President is inside."

While Mutt and Rip Cord keep up a steady conversation with their machine guns, you and the rest of the team skirt the perimeter looking for a weak spot. But COBRA guards are everywhere.

"We can't wait around! Gas 'em!" Flint yells.

Turn to page 6.

A voice, calm and cruel, comes over the ball-room's PA system: "This is the recorded voice of COBRA Commander, the last voice you will ever hear," it says. "My agents have overpowered the American guards and have sealed off every possible escape route."

The lights flash back on. The faces around the room are tense and sweaty. Except for the faces of your teammates—they're ready to spit bullets.

"We have gathered all of you tonight to partake in the culmination of COBRA's struggle to take over the world—not in slow and costly battles, but in one brilliant explosion. You are now trapped in a room with our robot assassin. In a few moments, he will be detonated and every one of your countries will come under my control. Good-bye."

Your eyes scan the room as you mutter to yourself, "Okay, Hotshot, let's see if you're as good as your name."

You look at the French, the Russians, the Germans...and you can't tell a thing from their faces. Any one of them could be the robot. But then you remember that the Argentine President was the last to arrive—just before this party got ugly.

Time is running out. What are you going to do?

....

If you think El Presidente is the robot, isolate him *on page 62.*

If you're not sure who the robot is, move the U.S. President to a safer location *on page 33.*

"I am not a robot," El Presidente says. "I am a man, a man who has worked all of his life for his country."

"Save it for the voters," Mutt snaps.

"Please—listen to me. I am an old man, a very ill man with not many months to live," El Presidente says. "COBRA knew this. Their Major Bludd came to me with a hideous plan to defile the dreams of these peace talks. When I refused to help him, he kidnapped my wife and three children. I had no choice but to submit to the operation."

"What operation?" Flint asks.

"COBRA implanted explosives in my stomach. They plan to detonate me tomorrow when all of the world leaders sit down for the peace talks," El Presidente says. "I would die soon anyway, so for me it doesn't matter..."

Without listening to any more, you grab a frequency transmitter and jam all the radio frequencies COBRA could use to explode the bomb. Then you rush El Presidente to the hospital, where the explosives are removed.

In the hospital all seven of you agree: You don't care how many strings Hawk has to pull to make it happen—you're heading straight for sunny Argentina to find El Presidente's family, as soon as you can get transport home!

THE END

With all of you aboard, Mutt is driving the one-ton truck toward the Rooster Mansion, wearing his ready-for-action smile.

"The Rooster Mansion," Flint says grimly. "The metal rooster at the top of the roof is really a machine-gun turret. But no one's had to use it lately because of the wall. Ten feet high, with broken glass imbedded in the bricks and stones. It's Band-Aid heaven."

"You want me to jump in, Flint?" Rip Cord asks.

"You're out of this one," Flint says. "You pull sentry duty on the outside and watch our rear. Snow Job, you're the diversion at the front gate. I don't care what you do, just so it pulls every guard from his post."

"This ought to get their attention, Snow Job, old buddy. It's my handy-dandy rubber vomit." Airtight chuckles and throws the chunky latex toy in Snow Job's lap.

"We need something uglier than that, Snow Job, because while you're out front, we'll be going over the wall," Flint says. "Once we're in, Mutt does his obedience-training act on the guard dogs."

The truck pulls to a stop.

"Let's go!" Blowtorch shouts, opening the flap on the back of the truck.

Turn to page 45.

"Snow Job!" you yell. "Stop him!"

Snow Job glares at you for a second, then clamps on his skis and shoves off. The man in front has a lead, but he's taking a curved, zigzag course down the steep mountain. Snow Job skis straight, making up time and picking up speed.

Suddenly Snow Job skids to a stop. Time for his biathlon training to take over. He raises his rifle and fires a warning shot into the snowbank below. Suddenly fifty tons of snow break loose and crash down on top of the skier, burying him in the avalanche.

"What if that isn't COBRA's robot?" you say to the rest of the Joe Team on top of the mountain.

You look at one another for a long second. Then the snowdrift far below you erupts like a volcano. Snow shoots high into the sky. The explosives which were buried in the skiing robot spray a fine powder all over the slopes.

Later you find out all the crucial details. The robot was posing as a clerk on the French minister's staff. He'd been hired by a COBRA agent who had infiltrated the French government.

So now that the President is safe, your job is over. There's nothing left for you to do except go home to the Pit—until the next time America needs the services of G.I. Joe!

THE END

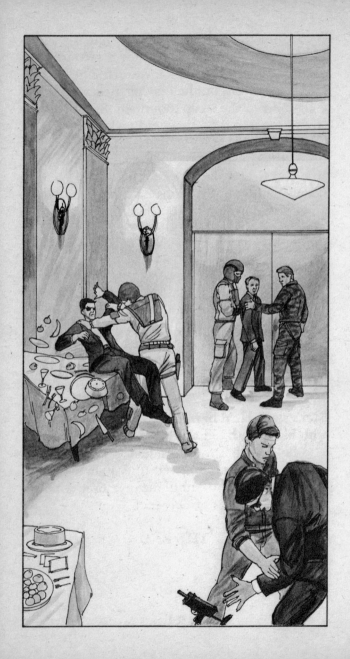

As long as you carry a United States Army ID, your first duty is to protect your Commander-in-Chief. If you blow that job, you'd better plan a career as an accountant.

"Let's get the President out of here *fast*," you say.

"I agree with you, buddy," Snow Job says. "But his secret service agents are wrapped around him tighter than a chestnut shell."

"Well, let's go reason with them," Flint says, rolling up his sleeves and marching toward the secret service.

When you're about four feet from the President, six secret service agents aim their revolvers at you. They're just doing their job—*or are they?* Who says COBRA can't disguise a robot as a secret service agent? You can't trust anyone.

A quick karate chop and you disarm one of the agents. Blowtorch grabs the suit of another and sends him flying into the table of cakes and fresh fruit. Flint launches two more into the orchestra as Airtight and Rip Cord grab the President. Then, with your guns firing, you escort the President out of the ballroom—forcibly.

. . . .

Turn to page 8.

Chattering rats lead the way as the Crimson Guard drag you down to a large room under the fort. Two of your *deadliest* enemies await you there—Destro and the Baroness. You look around the room filled with every ancient instrument of torture ever invented.

"Looks like you've got 'em all, except for some army training films," you say.

"Could we dispense with your macho humor and just get down to the torture?" the Baroness says.

Destro unlocks your handcuffs and opens the door of the tall metal box. The box is shaped vaguely like a human form. It swings open on hinges, and inside you see that the front and back are both lined with steel spikes.

"This is known as the Iron Maiden," the Baroness explains. "Messy, but quickly over. Or perhaps the rack is a better test of...your sense of humor, shall we say."

You can see no pleasure in the Baroness's eyes. For her, there is no fun or any meaning to this game. She is only a machine that must do evil—for reasons that even she no longer knows.

"Choose your death, Hotshot," the Baroness says. "Lady Jaye will get what's left."

· ·

If you choose the Iron Maiden, turn to page 55.

If you'd rather be put on the rack, turn to page 70.

On the faces of the world leaders you can see confusion, frustration, and anger, mixed liberally with sweat. It's rolling down their foreheads and cheeks.

"Hot enough for you?" Flint jokes with an interpreter from Finland.

"I'm used to it," the interpreter says with a smile.

Flint laughs, too, laying his hand on the young man's shoulder.

Five shots ring out as window glass scatters across the room. The first shot takes off the young man's head. The others remove his arms, legs, and central processing unit. The interpreter twitches, showering the room with frayed wires and electrical sparks.

You rush over to the robot and start searching for the explosive device. Its legs are packed with explosives, and the detonator is in the head. Your hands fly, cutting and pulling wires, smashing microchips.

"Next time COBRA builds an undetectable robot, they'd better remember to put in some sweat glands," Flint says.

Finally, you look up at Flint and say, "It's over."

THE END

The Chateau Noire is somebody's idea of the modern-day glass house. It doesn't have windows—it has whole walls of dark-tinted glass. Resting on a plateau at the peak of a ski slope, it looks like a dark crystal embedded in the white mountain.

You and your teammates are heading up a winding road to throw a few stones at this glass house. And you're going to use the firepower of an Abrams tank for your slingshot.

"I wish Bazooka was here," Mutt says at the controls.

"Just hold her steady, Mutt," Flint says. "We should be coming to the first security gate in a minute. After we crash that, there's no turning back. Security forces will close in from behind."

"The first fence is no sweatski. It's the second one—a mile farther up—that's the killer," Mutt says.

"By the time we hit the second fence, Rip Cord will parachute down and knock out the fence's laser defense system," Airtight says.

"And if not?" you say, asking for Flint's contingency plan.

"Then we cook faster than a microwave oven," Flint replies.

Turn to page 47.

"I worked as a dogcatcher for the pound one summer," you tell Mutt. "I know how to handle dogs."

"Well, good," Mutt says, helping you down the rope to the ground. "Of course, wolves are a little trickier."

"Wolves?" you say.

"Smile when you say that. Wolves like it when people smile," Mutt says. "Just do everything I do and things will be cool."

Mutt stares at the growling pack. You stare at the growling pack. Mutt reaches into his jacket. You reach into your jacket. Mutt pulls out a five-pound steak. You pull out a .38 caliber pistol . . . just in case. Mutt drops the steak at his feet.

"The leader will come for it first," Mutt says quietly.

The leader, gray and wary, inches forward toward the meat. It chomps a few bites and then lays down at Mutt's feet. Following the leader, all the wolves lay down.

"How did you do that?" you ask. "Hypnotism?"

"No, I soaked the meat in phenobarbital," Mutt says. "This big fellow is gonna sleep for an hour and the others will watch over him. Let's go."

Turn to page 56.

"Let *me* operate on him," Blowtorch says, reaching for his laser torch. "I guarantee you we'll know in five seconds if 'Mr. Undetectable' here is flesh and blood or circuits and plastic."

"Wait! What are you talking about?" the old man groans in a panic. "I am the President of Argentina!"

Mutt puts his face two inches from the old man. "We don't care if you say you're the President of Oz, pal. If you're working for COBRA, I'll bite your arm off!"

"I *am* a COBRA agent, but I am begging you to help me before it's too late!" El Presidente sobs.

Turn to page 29.

Before you can even approach another worker, Werner runs toward you, pushes open the other door, and points you toward the drinking fountain. As you press a button on the machine, a small robotic arm hands you a cup. It makes you laugh.

"There are so many machines here, it is good to hear real laughter for a change," someone behind you says.

You turn to face a young German woman. Her blond hair is tied in pigtails, and her bright blue eyes are circled with heavy black eye makeup.

"You are new. Do you come from far away?" she asks.

"Not far," you say, watching the small arm in the drinking fountain hand her a cup. "Do they ever put all these parts together?"

"What do you mean?" she asks, suddenly looking away.

"Do they ever build whole robots in the factory?" you ask.

"It is a robot factory," she says with a shrug. Then she turns her head and points with her eyes to a wall that has no door. "Be careful," she whispers. "The walls have ears."

···
Turn to page 59.

There's got to be time to check one more room. After all, what are thirty seconds when you're looking for a robot that's going to blow away world leaders?

You rush to the end of the hall and open a big wooden door slowly. It's black and silent inside the room. You step in cautiously.

Suddenly the lights come on. The room isn't empty. It's filled with Russian soldiers. They're shouting something in Russian, and then one of them steps forward holding a birthday cake with candles.

They were expecting someone else. And they're as surprised to see you as you are to see them. But they've got more guns than you do, so you're their prisoner.

A few hours later a Russian general, General Tarkinov, is speaking to an American general on the phone.

"Thank you, General," Tarkinov says. "I just wanted to check with you before I took appropriate actions."

Tarkinov hangs up and smiles at you. "My friend," he tells you, "General Brooker says there is no covert G.I. Joe activity in Geneva during the peace talks. You will have to tell me the truth about who you really are. We know you're not a G.I. Joe!"

Turn to page 50.

After lunch, you return to work. Werner is in good spirits. He must have had lunch at the beer hall. He grabs your arm and begins telling you sick robot jokes.

You're so busy trying to follow his German that you don't notice what's happening. A small disturbance at the front of the factory has become a large disruption. All of the machines are shutting down. And all of the workers are flocking to where the plant officials are arguing with two people.

"This plant must shut down immediately," a tall man with glasses as thick and black as his mustache announces in an official voice. "There is a contagious infection in this town, and everyone must be treated at once."

Turn to page 86.

Blowtorch carries his flamethrower in combat position through the halls of the palace. Up staircases...down wood-paneled halls. One hall leads endlessly to another. There are three floors of bedrooms—each one decorated to please a king. But every room in the palace is empty.

"I'm beginning to think we're doing the right thing at the wrong place," Blowtorch says. "We should be tripping over guards, soldiers, alarms, and diplomats. I've been through carwashes with more security than this!"

You motion to Blowtorch to freeze. There's a light under a door. You open the door slowly and peek in.

"There's an old man lying in bed," you whisper. "It's the Argentine president and he's fast asleep."

"Anyone else?" Blowtorch asks.

"Two servants. One of them is sleeping in a chair by the bed. The other one's nodding off by the door. No one's armed, and there's not a robot in sight."

Blowtorch looks at you and scratches his head.

"I don't get it," he says. "So far this isn't a job for the G.I. Joe Team—it's a scene from *Sleeping Beauty*. Only problem is—neither one of us looks like Prince Charming."

....

If you want to forget this place and come back later, turn to page 66.

If you want to try to wake El Presidente, turn to page 51.

42

"Doc, if you can save us the trouble of coming down hard on the old guy, you're welcome to try," you say as Airtight unlocks the door to the meeting room.

"Thank you. I'll do my best," the doctor says confidently.

The doctor is in the room only a few seconds when the room explodes. The fiery blast sends you flying into the walls.

Turn to page 54.

Some people know how to draw attention to themselves, and some people don't. Snow Job does. After the rest of you hop out, he aims the truck toward the front gate of the Rooster Mansion like a battering ram. The Russian guards don't wait to see what he's going to do next. They start firing at the truck with everything they can get their hands on. Just before the truck hits the wall, Snow Job spins the wheel and the truck tips and rolls over and over.

Did Snow Job walk away from that one? There's no time to be a spectator. Airtight launches his grapples and you, Flint, Blowtorch, and Mutt follow him up the rope.

The glass in the wall glimmers in the sunlight—like the sparkle inside a shark's jaws.

You're on top of the wall and not a guard in sight. Everything is going smoothly—for about five seconds. Then—trouble! There's something no one told you about—a little improvisation on the Russians' part. Five feet away from the wall you just climbed is another security fence. It's electrified, and there's barbed wire running across the top of it. And in between the first wall and the electric fence are packs of wild dogs pacing back and forth!

If you like dogs, turn to page 37.
If you're afraid of dogs, turn to page 25.

45

No two G.I. Joes are alike, but running through each of you is a shared philosophy: When someone tells you not to do something, do it as fast as you can.

That's why you can't keep away from the door Werner told you was forbidden. You wait for your moment, like a diver standing at the edge of the high board, waiting for the wind to calm just long enough.

Now! You pick the lock, swing the door open, and close it behind you, barely stirring the air.

You're in a cramped, stale room, lit by one bare bulb hanging from the ceiling. It takes a couple of seconds for your eyes to adjust and then you start looking for the robot.

There, lying beneath a blanket on a small wood-and-canvas cot, is the motionless figure of a man. He has the face of Lord Reginald Pemberton, the British junior ambassador who disappeared this week. His eyes open quickly and his head rises.

"This robot even has bloodshot eyes!" you say out loud.

··

Turn to page 7.

46

Everything is going along as planned. The tank smashes over the first fence as though it were made of aluminum instead of steel. Immediately, French security forces—armed jeeps and light trucks—are hot on your tail.

Mutt bounces you along on target for the second fence.

"Remind me never to complain about New York City taxi drivers again," Airtight cracks.

"You want to take over, wiseguy?" Mutt says.

Rip Cord is not in sight—but that's as planned, too. He's a HALO jumper—high altitude–low opening. He won't open his chute until he's practically touching ground.

"There's our CARE package dropping from the sky," Snow Job says, spotting Rip Cord.

"Hey, Flint, trouble!" Blowtorch says. "Look at that. Rip Cord's drifting. The wind is going to blow him away from the target. He'll never knock out the laser security in time!"

"Second fence coming up. What do I do, guys?" Mutt asks.

If you think Mutt should swerve and take a side road, turn to page 63.

If you think it's safe to smash through the gate, turn to page 57.

You're heading down another hall and suddenly you hear voices. You don't know what they're talking about, but you know Russian when you hear it. So you jump into the nearest closet and pull the door shut.

The voices pass. But when you try to leave the closet, you can't open the door. This booby-trapped house has tricked you again! The closet begins to close in on you. The back pushes you closer against the locked door. You pull on the doorknob and it comes off in your hand.

"Who built this place, Boris Karloff?" you ask yourself as you quickly jam your rifle between the closet door and the moving back wall.

The pressure finally punches your rifle through the door, and a little sweat-grunt-sweat on your part opens the door. You're free again, but time has run out. You've got to meet the rest of the Joe Team outside in thirty seconds. And you haven't found a thing!

If you want to follow the plan and meet the other G.I. Joes outside, turn to page 61.

If you want to look around a little longer, turn to page 40.

48

"I've got a pretty good idea where the limo's heading," you tell Flint. "There's a party at the American embassy."

"Let's get a chopper down here. We've got a party to crash!" Flint barks into his radio.

Five minutes later, the team scrambles out of a helicopter and heads for the front door of the embassy.

"Looks like an ordinary party. Not a sign of COBRA," Flint says, his eyes checking all directions at once.

"I'm gonna stay outside and scout around," Mutt says. He scratches the spotted mongrel's ears and then adds, "I hate parties."

"Hey, you boys have invitations?" asks one of the spit-and-polish guards who stops you at the front door.

Airtight cocks his M-16 and points the barrel right at the guard's nose. "Can you read my invitation, Corporal, or do you need more light?" he asks.

You rush to the ballroom, where the party is in full swing. The leaders of every important country in the world are in the room. El Presidente has just been wheeled in. Smiling, the American President comes to greet him. And then the lights go out.

"We got here just in time. Now the party's really starting," Rip Cord calls to you.

....

Turn to page 28.

The Russians hold you prisoner for a week. They know as well as you that General Brooker is lying through his teeth. But if you eliminated all the lying from politics, it just wouldn't be the same fun game.

Your life at the Rooster Mansion follows a calm routine. You're well fed, and in the afternoon you even get an exercise period outside. The guards don't watch you, because they're pretty sure you're not going anywhere. To get out, you'd have to face the electric fence, the wolves, and the glass wall again—unarmed and alone.

The guards must not watch the sky either. They don't see the brown silhouette sweep down from the blue Swiss horizon and hover above your head.

It's a helicopter, with Flint in the pilot's seat and Snow Job throwing the ladder down to you while firing rounds with his machine gun.

Turn to page 64.

Just as you and Blowtorch are about to step into El Presidente's room, one of the servants steps out. His face runs through every emotion in the book when he sees the two of you.

"Who are you and what are you doing on Argentine property?" the servant demands angrily.

"Since we've got the artillery, we'll ask the questions," Blowtorch snaps back. "Where is everybody?"

"Everyone has gone to the big party at the United States embassy," the servant says.

"So why didn't El Presidente go?" you ask.

"El Presidente has suffered an accident," the servant says. "Two days ago, while he was skiing, his appendix burst. He fell and rolled many times down the mountain. He was rushed to the hospital, where his appendix was removed. He must not be disturbed, because he has vowed to go to the peace talks tomorrow—even in his weak condition."

"We're not going to disturb him. I just want to make sure his head isn't attached with nuts and bolts," you say, smiling at Blowtorch.

"Juan, I hear voices. Who is out there?" calls a hoarse voice from inside the bedroom.

Turn to page 82.

Destro takes a .45 automatic from his belt and tosses it to you. "Kill her," he says, pointing to Lady Jaye.

You know what you have to do. Without blinking, you aim the gun at Lady Jaye and squeeze the trigger.

Click!

"The gun's empty," you say, tossing it at Destro. "You made me look like a fool!"

"*I* would have been the fool if I had given you a loaded gun for your first test," Destro says.

If you keep pretending you're on COBRA's side, maybe they'll drop their guard just for a minute. That's all the time you'll need to spring Lady Jaye and hot-foot it out of here.

"Let me show you, once and for all, how I feel about this G.I. Jerk," you say, spitting on the ground in front of Lady Jaye. You walk toward her menacingly. "She's the one who got me into this mess—"

"Okay," the Baroness says, giving you a clip of ammo. "You've made your point. Now take your friend down to one of the torture cells and lock her up. And no tricks."

Turn to page 72.

Too bad your Joe Team didn't realize the doctor was the robot assassin. You allowed him to enter the meeting room and blow up all of the world's leaders. For that you are dishonorably discharged and disgraced. The *National Inquirer* hounds you for the rest of your lives, printing articles about the G.I. Shmoes. And each of you leads a humiliating life.

Flint becomes a counselor at a summer camp for rich kids, where he must spend the last two weeks every August begging their parents for tips.

Blowtorch is out of work for five years and finally must take a job in his cousin's factory—testing lighter fluid formulas.

Mutt finds work as a gravedigger at a pet cemetery.

Snow Job loses his hair and tries to become the first man to ski down the Grand Canyon.

Airtight appears in television commercials for the elderly, promoting the benefits of a chewable antacid.

And you, Hotshot, are stuck in a traveling carnival, lighting the fuses on the cannon that sends Egor the Human Cannonball flying through the air.

THE END

You nod toward the Iron Maiden, avoiding Lady Jaye's eyes.

Destro starts backing you into the metal coffin at gunpoint, when suddenly there's a loud explosion upstairs.

"Chain them to the wall!" the Baroness shouts to the guards behind her.

You and Lady Jaye are chained as Destro and the Baroness run up the stairs. The guards follow them and a steel door closes over the opening to the room. You hear fighting above. It's got to be the Joe Team making a house call. A few minutes later, the commotion ends.

Silence. You and Lady Jaye look at each other and rattle your chains in frustration. Who won?

That's when the steel door to the torture room opens again, and the G.I. Joe Team comes down the stairs. In seconds you're free, running out of the fortress toward a truck.

"The Baroness and Destro?" you shout, hopping in.

Duke shrugs his shoulders.

"What about the robot assassin?" Lady Jaye asks.

Turn to page 87.

Flint leads the way through the second fence. Each of you knows the drill. You run straight ahead for cover without looking back. Maybe the Joe Team is behind you, maybe Smokey the Bear. But get out of sight and undercover fast and first.

"Company's coming," Airtight says, scouting around. "Hope you all like Russian dressing on your salad."

You look up and see a platoon of Russian guards marching past the bush you're hiding in. Mutt sticks out his leg, the first soldier falls, and it's dominoes time.

In seconds the Russians are knocked out, stripped, and tied up. In their place—and in their uniforms—are five of America's finest G.I. Joes.

"Let's split up," Blowtorch says. "We've got to find that robot in ten minutes. That's how long it'll take the main guardhouse to miss these guys and come looking for us."

"Right," Flint says. "You guys get back here in ten minutes *exactly* or the bus leaves without you. And remember: Every inch of this place is booby-trapped.

"What'll it be, Hotshot? Do you want the top floor or the bottom?"

....

If you want to cover the main floor, turn to page 77.

If you want to check the upstairs living quarters, turn to page 17.

"Smash through the gate!" you yell. The tank hits the fence at top speed. If you're going out, you might as well go out in a blaze of laser glory.

But the second fence crumbles when you hit it, same as the first. Somehow, good old Rip Cord got to the laser control box in time.

As you pull up to the Chateau Noire, you notice that there's no security fence on the other side of the mountain. But why should there be? There's no road access from that side—only two thousand feet of the steepest slopes in Switzerland. From the Chateau Noire, you can look down on a half-dozen ski resorts located below.

The first thing you see when you arrive is a man on skis arguing with the ski slope attendant just outside the chateau. You can't tell what they're arguing about. But when the man notices you, he pushes the attendant down and takes off down the slick slope.

Could this be COBRA's robot? You'd better decide fast, because he's getting away.

If you think the Joe Team should follow the man down the slope, turn to page 31.

If you don't think the skier is the robot, enter the Chateau Noire on page 83.

Everyone leaps to catch the watch before it falls. But just before it hits the floor, the dog comes up with it in his teeth. He carries it dutifully over to Mutt, who's standing in the doorway with his M-16 trained on Juan.

"Mutt! How did you get in?" Flint asks.

"No big deal," Mutt answers. "There were only twenty COBRA agents outside. Hey—good-looking eats."

Mutt retires to the food table, handing you the watch as he passes. And you join the rest of your teammates, who are escorting the Argentine president out.

"COBRA must have made up the rumor about the robot assassin. It threw us off the track—and covered up your phony skiing accident," Blowtorch explains to El Presidente.

"But when we breached the Beuler Palace tonight, COBRA knew we were close," you say. "So they brought you here and stepped up their timetable. Why not? All the world leaders were present at this party."

While you talk you remove the detonator from the wristwatch. Then you give the watch back to El Presidente.

"You keep it," El Presidente says, handing it back to you through his limo window. He smiles. "I can see that knowing when the time is going to run out is much more important to you."

THE END

You move slowly toward the wall with no door. When you're sure no one is watching, you begin to feel for a secret entrance. The surface is completely smooth. Suddenly your arm crosses the beam of an electronic eye, and part of the wall slides open.

The room you enter is dark and filled with all shapes and sizes of robot parts hanging on hooks from the ceiling. And there, on a long table in the middle of the room, is the answer to your question. A robot is lying on the table, completely assembled except for one leg.

This is COBRA's robot, all right. They've already decided on its identity. And only COBRA would have created a robot with the face of Lord Reginald Pemberton, a junior ambassador from Great Britain and a distant relative of the Queen. Three days ago, Lord Reg, as he likes to be called, disappeared into thin air. Now it looks as if COBRA is planning to have a new Lord Reg show up at the peace talks in Switzerland—an ambassador packed with explosives.

You think for a moment. You could just detonate this baby. Or you could send it on a mission for your side.

If you decide to reprogram the robot so it will destroy COBRA headquarters, turn to page 9.

If you think it's safer to remove the explosives and then get out of the factory fast, turn to page 20.

59

It takes all of the strength of the Baroness and Destro to turn your torture wheel of misfortune. However, it takes all of their attention, too.

While they're busy with the rack, your two torturers don't see Lady Jaye lift herself by the arms like a gymnast on the rings. Bent in half, she reaches up with her feet for an old and familiar friend left on the wall from centuries past. She picks a crossbow from its hook. And when it's in her manacled hands, she shouts, "Hold it right there or I'll nail you snakes to the wall!"

Turn to page 73.

You go to meet the Joe Team a sweaty mess from your wrestling match with the booby traps in this house. And the others look like they've gotten the wrong end of the stick too.

"Hey, there wasn't one single smoke detector in that place. It's a firetrap," Blowtorch says gravely. Blowtorch knows fire and he respects its power above all else.

"Don't sweat the small stuff, Blowtorch," Airtight says. "I almost got sliced in two opening a bedroom closet."

"I had my share of fun too," you grumble.

"What is this place? A fun house for killjoys?" Mutt says. "How can the Russians live in a place like this?"

"It's more fun than Russian TV," Flint says. "Okay, we've come up empty-handed. No robot. Maybe it's there and we missed it. But more likely, the robot is already on his way to the peace talks."

"The first session starts in two hours. We've got to hustle," Blowtorch says.

So you gladly scramble off the Rooster Mansion grounds and over the wall of glass again. Outside, you rendezvous with Rip Cord and Snow Job and head for the Swiss government building where the peace talks are about to begin.

Turn to page 27.

"Get everybody to the other side of the room. El Presidente's the robot!" you yell to Flint. "El Presidente, move away from your aides," you say, approaching the old man in the wheelchair.

Suddenly one of the aides pulls a revolver. "You cannot treat El Presidente de Argentina this way," she says.

"That's not El Presidente! It's a robot!" you yell. But Snow Job's M-16 barks louder. He fires a short burst at the punch bowl. The shattering glass grabs everyone's attention.

"Wait!" El Presidente says, standing up weakly. "If you want me that badly, I will be your prisoner."

But Juan, El Presidente's trusted servant, wraps his arm around El Presidente's throat and points a .38 at his head. El Presidente looks at Juan with surprise and then with fear.

"Fear? How can a robot be afraid?" you mutter.

"Hey—I get it now," Blowtorch says. "He's not a robot. There *is* no robot—but there *is* a bomb. I'll bet COBRA implanted one in his stomach when they opened him up for that phony appendix operation."

Turn to page 69.

Mutt steers hard, and the tank does a ninety-degree turn up a side road.

"Great scott! What's that?" Flint shouts.

But there's no time to talk about it. There's only time to collide with it—head on. *BOOM!!*

An enormous explosion rocks the tank and kicks up a large chunk of the mountain.

Except for a few bashed kneecaps, you and the others are okay. You climb out of the tank to inspect the smoldering, twisted pile of steel you've just driven over.

"It used to be a limo," Flint says. "It was pulling out of the Chateau Noire from a side entrance."

Suddenly all of you start to grin at once. There's only one thing that could explode with that much force.

"We just knocked out COBRA's robot, guys," you say.

"Nailed him before he left the starting gate," Blowtorch adds with a smile. "This is our lucky day!"

But who was in the car? Later you find out that there were two people: the French foreign minister's secretary and a chauffeur. You know that one of them was a robot time bomb. But was the other a COBRA operative—or an innocent victim? That, you'll never know for sure.

THE END

"The robot?" you ask as soon as you're on board the helicopter.

"We pulled its plug," Snow Job says. "Mission accomplished. The world is safe from COBRA once again—for a while."

"Regards from General Brooker," Flint says with a smile.

"He's off my Christmas list," you say.

"No, he came through," Flint says. "When he found out what the Russians planned to do with you back in Russia, Brooker told me three words: 'Get him somehow.' By the way, what held you up in the mansion?"

"I stopped for some birthday cake," you say with a weary smile.

Flint points the helicopter toward the secret Swiss airstrip. Your job is finished. You're all going home. The Pit is calling you back.

THE END

You search frantically through the pieces of the robot. You're sure they put an auto-destruct loop in it somewhere—so that if something happens to the robot, it blows up anyway. The trouble is, you don't know how long before it goes. Five minutes? One minute? Less?

Your fingers follow circuits and chips the way other people trace highways on road maps. Bingo! There's the timer. No time to be neat—you rip it out with a yank.

"Good work, Hotshot," Blowtorch says. "But that Belgian fruitcake is still holding the President hostage. And we've only got two minutes left! Let's get in there."

But just as you burst into the conference room, you hear a familiar sound. *Whap-whap-whap.* It's the beat of a chopper's props. You look out the window and smile at Flint's helicopter hovering outside.

The Belgian ambassador is still raving. "Peace talks!" he snorts. "I wouldn't play with you loonies in a *sandbox*!"

"Mr. Ambassador," you say as you help him into the copter and a waiting straitjacket, "have a very pleasant flight home."

THE END

Now you understand how old man Beuler could get lost forever in his own house. The place is so big that after an hour of trying, you and Blowtorch still haven't found your way out.

You wander into a room filled with suits of armor. The walls are covered with stuffed animal heads. By now, nothing about this house could surprise you. But the sight of a short man wearing white pants and a white jacket comes as a complete shock. He is sitting peacefully in an armchair, admiring the roaring fireplace.

The three of you stare at one another for a second.

"Hey, ice cream man, how do we get out of here?" Blowtorch finally says.

"I'll show you the fastest way out," the small man says. He grabs a knife from beneath his cushioned chair and charges at you like a missile. His eyes gleam—but nothing shines as bright as the gleaming COBRA insignia on the onyx handle of his knife. Your attacker strikes. His arms are quick and strong—but they're also short. The knife misses your head by an inch.

Turn to page 21.

"I don't think the robot's in there yet. So let's seal the room tight," you say.

"Right, but someone's got to explain to all those VIPs why they've just been placed in quarantine," Blowtorch says.

"No problem. I'll show you how it's done," Airtight says, pulling you into the conference room with him.

"Ladies and gentlemen, sorry to interrupt your peace talks," Airtight begins. "But I lost my pet rattlesnake this morning. Anybody seen him? Hahaha! Just kidding. Now that you're all listening—the truth is there's been a little bomb scare. We know that this room is safe, so until we can secure the outside area, for your own safety, no one goes in or out of this room. If you need anything, the telephone in this room will ring direct to our checkpoint phone outside."

After that, Airtight leaves the room in utterly shocked silence.

"You just got to know how to put people at ease. That's what it's all about, Hotshot," Airtight says.

Turn to page 71.

"You are quick," Juan says. "Finally, you discover there is no robot. COBRA has outsmarted you this time."

Juan throws his .38 at your feet. "Keep it as a souvenir," he says with a laugh. "El Presidente has enough explosives in his stomach to blow up half of Geneva. He was set to go off during the peace talks tomorrow, but I'll have to press the button now."

Juan grabs the wristwatch on El Presidente's arm, and suddenly you realize the watch must be the detonator.

"If you push that button, you will kill yourself as well," Flint says.

El Presidente gasps as Juan tightens his grip. "Don't be a fool, Juan. Think of your family," he says.

"COBRA is my family!" Juan shouts.

"Push the button and you can forget about this year's family reunion," Airtight cracks.

Out of nowhere, a snarling black and white streak flies through the air. It's the dog Mutt dragged in. The dog goes right for Juan's hand and Juan drops the watch, grabbing his hand in pain. Your eyes go wide. If the watch hits the floor too hard, this party is going to end with a loud bang.

Turn to page 58.

"I'll take the rack," you say. "I could use a stretch. And besides, I always wanted to play in the NBA."

The Baroness gives you a cold, bored look and motions for Destro to strap you onto the rack. Destro's hands hold you tighter than the rope he uses to tie you down. After he's done with you, he pushes Lady Jaye against a wall and chains her arms in cuffs.

"Baroness, I'll make you a bet," you say. "Give me everything you've got, but if I survive the rack, Lady Jaye stays out of the Iron Maiden."

"Why should I agree to anything like that?" the Baroness says.

"Because you're wondering what I've got up my sleeve," you say confidently.

"I don't make deals with G.I. Joes," the Baroness replies. "We'll just see if you still have a sleeve when I've finished with you."

Then she and Destro begin to turn the ancient creaking wheel that pulls the ropes.

Turn to page 60.

You're back outside the meeting room for only thirty seconds when the checkpoint phone rings. Mutt grabs it.

"Hello," Mutt says. "Oh, hello, Mr. Ambassador."

What follows is a series of "Uh-huh's" on Mutt's part. Then he slams the phone down and bangs his fist on the desk. "That was the ambassador from Belgium. That jerk's gone scrambled eggs in there! He's so worked up about a possible bomb that he's taken the President as hostage! He says if we don't get him out of here by helicopter within thirty minutes, he's going to kill our President. He tied their neckties together and he's holding a gun to the President's head."

"Gentlemen, I think I can be of use to you," says a man waiting nearby in the lobby. He's carrying a leather bag and stroking his trimmed black beard. "I'm the Belgian ambassador's physician. The Ambassador has a medical history of—shall we say—irrational behavior. But I have something here that will calm him down . . . if you'll allow me to give him the injection," the doctor says, looking at you.

If you want to let the doctor go in and give the injection, turn to page 43.

If you don't, turn to page 11.

71

As soon as you're out of the Baroness's sight, Lady Jaye smiles at you.

"It's a good thing Uncle Sam gave us that weight-sensitivity training for weapons," she says.

"Yeah, I knew the minute that gun hit my hand it wasn't loaded. It wasn't heavy enough," you say. "Look at this place. My guess is this 'facility' was used during the Spanish Inquisition."

"Ah, yes. That was a lovely time in Spain's past—when people were tortured and killed for not believing just what the state wanted them to believe," Lady Jaye says. "No wonder COBRA likes this place. Of course, if Destro's involved, it's probably being used as a weapons cache."

You lock Lady Jaye in one of the underground torture cells beneath the courtyard of the fort. "I'll be back tonight," you say. "We're checking out at midnight."

Turn to page 88.

"You've got us covered, but I've still got Hotshot right where I want him—under my thumb," the Baroness says.

That's all you want to take from these two. So you bang your wrists against the table to set off the mini-explosives concealed on your wristbands. The old ropes of the rack catch fire and disappear like tiny birthday candles in fast forward. You leap off the rack and join Lady Jaye.

"Which one of you wants to die?" Lady Jaye asks.

While Destro and the Baroness try to decide what to do, the burning ropes ignite other ropes, and the dry wood in the torture room also begins to burn.

"We've got to get out of here," Destro says. "Do I have to remind you that this room is directly beneath our ammunition storeroom?"

Too bad Destro didn't remind you a little sooner. The flames climb through the cracks to the ammo above. Then you all go through some major changes—from living legends to dead ducks.

Meanwhile, the Joe Team back in Germany finds COBRA's robot assassin. They disarm it before it can leave for the Geneva peace talks.

Afterward, back at the Pit, Hawk promises to move heaven and earth to find you and Lady Jaye. If only he knew—that's just what it will take.

THE END

You pull a small radio from a holster hidden on your back and recite a quick signal. "Lifeguard, this is swimmer," you say. "I'm ready to come out of the pool." Then you tell Lord Reg that it won't be long.

And it isn't very long before the door to Lord Reg's secret room opens—in fact, it's not long enough. In walk a dozen of COBRA's red-uniformed Crimson Guard. And with them is Destro and COBRA Commander himself.

COBRA Commander's eyes flash fire. "The nerve, the absolute nerve. What are you doing in here?" he shouts.

You try a little of your German on him but he interrupts you. "Knock it off," he snaps. "I can smell a G.I. Joe Team a mile away."

"They're probably closer than that by now," you say confidently.

The sound of a wall being plowed down by a tank announces the fact that the Joe Team is coming.

"I think I hear them knocking right now," you say.

COBRA Commander suddenly loses all control and leaps for your throat.

Turn to page 19.

"I'm on my way down!" Snow Job shouts, clamping on his skis. "You guys follow in the tank."

By the time you arrive, Snow Job has moved the President to safety. And he's dismantled COBRA's robot.

"Lucky for us the thing malfunctioned and fell down in the snow," Snow Job says. "But hurry, Hotshot! I uncovered its countdown clock and there are only twenty seconds before it blows!"

You give the robot a quick once-over and then laugh your head off.

"Relax," you say. "That isn't the countdown clock. It's just a sixty-second clock that keeps the robot's computer working. It'll recycle when it gets to zero."

You watch the sixty-second clock tick down to zero. And then the whole thing blows up in your face, wiping out the President and your entire team with it.

Maybe COBRA can't build a robot that won't fall apart—but they really know how to design a countdown clock that will fool even a hotshot like you!

THE END

The first room you check out on the main floor is enormous. It's a ballroom with a glass-slick dance floor and a two-ton crystal chandelier hanging from the ceiling.

There's not a sign of a robot, so you hurry across the dance floor. But you get a funny feeling in your stomach. Is it something you ate? Or is the floor really beginning to spin faster and faster? Suddenly the chandelier comes at you— like a wrecking ball!

You hit the floor. Not easy, since it's spinning faster than a carnival ride. You crawl, keeping low. The chandelier goes zipping over your head. But you grip the floor tightly and try to crawl straight for the door.

"What's that room for?" Mutt asks as you pass him in the hall.

"For people who want to take a spin around the dance floor," you say. "See you in five."

Turn to page 48.

"I say the robot's already in the meeting," you tell the Joe Team.

"Let's not take a chance," Flint says. "If the robot's in there, we've got to double-time it. Blowtorch, go down to engineering and turn up the heat in this building as high as it will go."

Airtight looks at Flint as if he's been out in the sun too long. "What's the plan?"

"Hotshot and I are going down to the conference room to find that robot," Flint says. "Snow Job, take Mutt and Rip Cord to cover you and get on the rooftop across the street. I want you to have a clear shot into the assembly."

"What do you want me to do?" Snow Job asks.

"I'm going to put my hand on someone's shoulder," Flint says to him. "And when I do, Mr. Olympic Biathlon, I want you to blow him away."

When you and Flint step into the room, it's like stepping into a steaming jungle. The heat is unbearable.

"Ladies and gentlemen," Flint announces. He walks around the circular table looking into the faces of the world leaders. "I'm sorry for your discomfort. We're having troubles with our boiler, but we're going to take care of it in just another minute."

....

Turn to page 35.

The Reinhardt Robotics Factory is a large, dirty old brick building. But inside it has modern equipment and a large crew cranking out artificial arms and legs.

"You want work? We have work," the plant manager says. He is a thin, sweaty man. He and Werner make a good drippy team.

So far, your disguise as a poor German laborer is working. And disguise is only your secondary specialty. You hope you're just as successful with your primary specialty— defusing explosives.

The manager explains that robotic arms are made in one part of the factory and robotic hands in another. You are assigned to work with Werner, putting them together.

Later that morning, you decide it's time to begin your investigation. "Where's the water fountain?" you ask casually. Werner points you toward a wall with two doors. You walk over and start to push one open.

"Not that door!" Werner shouts. "You are not allowed in that room."

So what big secret are they hiding behind door #1?

....
If you want to pump the other workers for information, turn to page 39.

If you want to see what's behind door #1, turn to page 46.

79

Your plane touches down on an airstrip wedged smack in the middle of Switzerland's snow-topped mountains. The beautiful and bustling city of Geneva is two hours away.

You, Flint, and the others carefully watch the faces passing you on the Geneva streets. You wonder how the tourists would feel if they knew that COBRA's robotic time bomb was walking around Geneva.

"Buy my flowers," a young woman calls. She has pigtails and is wearing traditional Swiss peasant clothing.

"Now, what would we do with flowers, pretty lady?" Snow Job answers.

"You can stick them in your ear, Joe," the woman says.

For the first time Flint smiles. "Team," he says, "meet Ellie Knudsen, our intelligence contact in Geneva. What's the latest, Ellie?"

"Well, Flint, we've narrowed it down to three possible contenders for Rat of the Month—Argentina, Russia, and France," Ellie says in a low voice. "Each of those countries has had some contact with COBRA recently. We don't know how deep the contact went—it could have been accidental. But my sources think the robot is hiding out among the diplomats from one of those three countries."

Turn to page 16.

Duke, Snake-Eyes, and Lady Jaye come in carrying parts of the robot. "Guess what Humpty Dumpty and your robot have in common?" Duke says to COBRA Commander.

"Here's a hint," you say. "You'll never get it back together again—not in time to beat us to the peace talks with the *real* Lord Reg."

"I told you from the beginning this was a dumb idea," Destro says. "You want to blow up world leaders? You get a plane and you drop a bomb. It's as simple as it is ugly."

"So are you," COBRA Commander snaps. Then he grabs Lord Reg by the throat. "Back off. We're getting out of here—or he dies!"

Turn to page 12.

You walk past Juan into El Presidente's bedroom. The gray-haired man lying in bed is only half awake. One look at his face tells you that he has been given many sedatives. Even though he's drugged, he's alert enough to be alarmed by your black-smeared faces. You can see the fear in his eyes.

"El Presidente, it was very important for us to see you," you say, trying to calm him. You pick up the old man's hand and feel that it is thin and bony—but it's warm and definitely made of real flesh. "We are very sorry to hear about your accident and hope that you recover quickly."

As you speak, Blowtorch lifts El Presidente's sheets and bedclothes.

"That's a first-class appendix scar," Blowtorch says. The two servants begin to stir, but Blowtorch's glare freezes them in their tracks.

"I don't remember about it," El Presidente says. "I was skiing. I felt a sharp pain in my head. Then I fell."

"El Presidente, don't you mean a pain in your side?" you ask.

But the old man slips off to sleep.

"Head—side—what's the difference?" Blowtorch says. "He's not our robot. Let's get out of here."

Turn to page 13.

"Ski bums. Won't stay off the slopes even when they're warned it's too icy," the ski attendant mutters as you and Flint lead the way into the Chateau Noire.

A French butler stops you in the entryway. You're not sure what he's saying, since you don't speak very much French. So you just assume he's saying "Make yourself at home." Which means you push past him and immediately start searching the place for signs of COBRA and their robot.

Snow Job, however, opens a sliding glass door and steps onto one of the chateau's glass balconies. He looks through a five-inch telescope that's set up for a view of the slope. He's still keeping an eye on the skier who had the argument with the slope attendant.

"Hey, Flint!" Snow Job yells. "That skier is heading like a bowling ball right for a group of people."

Flint comes out and Snow Job passes him the telescope.

"He's heading straight at the President's skiing party!" Flint shouts.

Turn to page 14.

"You can't fool me twice, Lady Jaye," you say. "What was going on back there?"

"We thought of a way of getting under COBRA's skin, right, Duke?" Lady Jaye says with a laugh.

"We knew there had to be some COBRA operatives in the plant," Duke says. "So Lady Jaye inoculated the regular workers with a harmless serum. But she gave the COBRA agents we recognized a special serum filled with a chemical homing device."

"So now the robot can track the COBRA agents back to headquarters," you say. "And when he gets inside, they'll celebrate the Fourth of July at close range."

"It's even better than that, toots," Lady Jaye says as she drives. "Do you know who happened to be in the factory? The Baroness herself. That COBRA ice cube stared me right in the eyes and didn't recognize me. So I gave her an extra dose for luck. Makes you wonder how smart COBRA's intelligence officers really are."

The next day, the TV news reports that an abandoned schoolhouse blew up shortly after midnight last night. You and your teammates howl when you hear that police suspect the bombing was the work of an inept terrorist group who just didn't know how to handle explosives!

THE END

"Yeah, and El Presidente is no robot—he's just a tired old man who needs a little R and R after an emergency operation," Blowtorch adds. "He's not going anywhere for a while."

That makes Snow Job laugh. "Oh, yeah? Well, a minute ago two guys carried El Presidente out of there in a wheelchair. They bundled him into a limo and sped off toward town."

"What's going on?" you say, feeling as if you've just found a KICK ME sign on your back.

"Maybe we're wrong about El Presidente. Maybe he *is* the robot," Blowtorch says to you.

....
If you want to search for the limo, turn to page 49.

If you think you're too late, get some sleep and then go on to the next villa on page 30 tomorrow morning.

85

Standing next to the man with the dark mustache is a nurse, an old, dumpy woman who long ago must have given up liking her job and her life.

"Everyone must have a shot or they will die," the nurse says sternly over the protests of the plant officials.

The plant workers line up, and the nurse checks all of them carefully before giving them a shot with a long, evil-looking syringe. You're suspicious of this whole operation, but you don't dare call attention to yourself. Reluctantly, you line up with the rest. When it's your turn, the nurse examines your throat, and as she does a look of understanding comes into your eyes. Instantly, she clamps a face mask over your nose and mouth and says, "Quarantine immediately."

The nurse and the government official drag you quickly out of the plant and into the car.

Turn to page 84.

You wait for Duke to answer Lady Jaye's question. Did they find the killer robot in time?

"Thanks to you two, we knew the robot was a dupe of Lord Reg," Duke says.

"Huh?" you say. "How'd you know that?"

"You're wearing a radio transmitter in your belt, remember?" Duke says. "We heard everything that went on in that German factory. We got the info to the Joe Team in Switzerland, and they stopped the robot before it exploded."

"Let's roll! This place is about to become a roman candle!" Bazooka shouts.

And as you drive away, one of COBRA's secret munition dumps becomes a loud and bright thing of the past.

THE END

That night, when there are only two guards on watch, you and Lady Jaye work your way out of the fortress. Lady Jaye neatly dispatches the guards while you steal a COBRA truck. All night long you drive across the Spanish desert.

A few days later, you are reunited with Duke and the rest of the Joe Team.

Duke is glad to see you, but he hides it well. "It's about time you showed up," he says. "While you two took a little vacation, we worked our tails off finding that robot bomb and knocking it out of commission!" He shakes his head and grins. "Some first mission, Hotshot. Looks like we're gonna have to give you another assignment." That's fine with you. You're ready!

THE END

Three seconds isn't a very long time—just long enough to put a few of the pieces together. COBRA substituted its robot assassin for the President of the United States! How and when? And where is the real President now?

If you get out of this mess, rescuing the President will probably be your next assignment, you think to yourself as you reach into the robot's wires to deactivate it.

But you can't. Three seconds isn't long enough—even for a hotshot like you. The robot glows red and then explodes like a geyser.

Back in the States, you, Flint, Snow Job, Blowtorch, Airtight, Mutt, and Rip Cord are given heroes' funerals—even though your mission was definitely blown!

THE END